Dear Parent:

This tale portrays a set of interactions common among young children. You are likely to find Cleo's "stretching" of the rules to suit herself quite familiar. You may have marveled that it's so easy for your child to understand and apply the rules of "good conduct" to others by strictly monitoring whether someone else is playing fair, taking turns, or sharing—while not applying the same rigorous standards to his or her own behavior! *Follow the Leader* gives you an opportunity to talk, indirectly, about this issue. One character's facile bending of the rules for her own sake may have you wondering aloud whether Cleo would do the same for others. Or, would the rules become iron-clad if the tables were turned?

In discussing Cleo's behavior, it is wise to keep any amusement to yourself and gently point out to your child the "unfairness" of the situation. But be prepared to hear the phrase "it's not fair" countless times in sibling and other family situations. Children understand the concept of fairness very well when it comes to defending their own positions. Rest assured, however, that your child is hardly unique in possessing this dubious skill. Gradually, maturation and your calm, patient reiteration of the universality of rules will have the desired effect.

Adele M. Brodkin, Ph.D.

D1366531

Visit Clifford at scholastic.com/clifford

ISBN 0-439-22464-0

Copyright © 2001 Scholastic Entertainment Inc. All rights reserved. Based on the CLIFFORD THE BIG RED DOG book series published by Scholastic Inc. TM & © Norman Bridwell. SCHOLASTIC, CARTWHEEL BOOKS, and associated logos are trademarks and/or registered trademarks of Scholastic Inc. CLIFFORD, CLIFFORD THE BIG RED DOG, CLIFFORD & COMPANY, and associated logos are trademarks and/or registered trademarks of Norman Bridwell.

Library of Congress Cataloging-in-Publication Data is available

10 9 8 7 6 5 4 3 2 1   01 02 03 04 05 06

Printed in the U.S.A.   24
First printing, July 2001

Scholastic

Clifford THE BIG RED DOG®

Follow the Leader

Adapted by Kalli Dakos

Illustrated by Carolyn Bracken and Sandrina Kurtz

**Based on the Scholastic book series
"Clifford The Big Red Dog"
by Norman Bridwell**

From the television script
"Follow the Leader" by Bob Carrau

Cartwheel
·B·O·O·K·S· ®

SCHOLASTIC INC.

New York   Toronto   London   Auckland   Sydney   Mexico City
New Delhi   Hong Kong

Clifford, T-Bone,
And Cleo, too,
Have to find something
Exciting to do.
"I'll be the leader,"
Cleo cries,
"In follow-the-leader.
Now follow me, guys."

T-Bone is second
And Clifford is third.
They must listen
To Cleo's every word.
"Now spin your tails
Just like mine.
Come on, T-Bone.
You're looking fine."

Then Clifford's tail
Spins in the air
And—oops!—trims a hedge
Into a square.

As the dogs move on
T-Bone claims,
"I think it's *my* turn
To lead the game."

A man is reading,
And a woman, too,
On a bench—uh-oh!—
What will Cleo do?
She zips underneath,
Then runs back out,
And T-Bone follows
Her all about.

Then Clifford crawls

Down beneath,

But the bench pops up,

And he's soon underneath....

It's on Clifford's head,
Sliding down his back
And off his tail.
It lands with a *whack!*...

It's where it was
A moment ago,
And the two readers
Don't even know
That they've been on
A slippery ride—
On a great big
Clifford-slide.

"Now step on this bridge!"
Cleo yells.
"Do whatever
The leader tells."

But T-Bone says,
"It's time *I* became
The leader of
This follow-me game."

"Forty-six things
I get to do.
Forty-six things
Are in the rules,"
Cleo says. "And I've
Only done three.
You'll get your turn,
Just wait and see."

She hops up the alley

And climbs into a box.

But when T-Bone tries,

He falls down like rocks.

"It must be *my* turn!"

T-Bone cries.

"No, mine's extra long,"

Cleo replies.

"I vote for T-Bone,"
Says Clifford. "I do."
And T-Bone yells,
"I vote for me, too!"
Then Clifford says,
"The voting is done.
T-Bone's the leader—
Two to one!"

T-Bone struts off,

"Okay, follow me."

But Cleo stands still,

"I do not agree."

"Keep leading," says Clifford.

"She'll follow, I know."

But as they walk away,

She says, "I won't go...

"Because I'm *still* the leader,
And they have to come back."
She dives into the box
Where it's dark and it's black.

Clifford and T-Bone

Pass a big truck,

Which then picks up Cleo,

Surprised by her luck.

"Hey, this is great!"
Cleo calls. "Now I'll go
To the swap meet—
It's the best place I know!"

When Cleo arrives
She looks all around
At the wonderful things
She sees on the ground.

"T-Bone would love
This squishy, soft chair.
But this nice chair would flatten
If Clifford sat there."

Then Cleo frowns:
"I think it's clear
My turn was too long.
I wish they were here."

"AHHHHHHHH!" she yells,

As two heads in fluff

Pop right up

In their fancy stuff.

T-Bone yells,

"We've been looking for you!"

And Cleo sighs,

"I've missed both of you, too."

"Now, follow the leader.

That's me," she calls.

But Clifford and T-Bone

Don't move at all.

Then Cleo stops short

And says, "No, not me.

T-Bone's the leader,

And now I agree."

They run up the seesaw,
And down the side.
But when Clifford gets on,
It's too small to ride!

T-Bone slides through a pipe

With Cleo behind,

And Clifford's tail

Is next in line.

"My turn is over,"
T-Bone says and sits down.
And Cleo yells, "Clifford!
Lead us around!
For it's good to take turns,
And it's good to play fair,
And to not make up rules,
And it's good to share."

T-Bone is third,

As places reverse.

Cleo is second,

And Clifford is first.

"I'll lead us home,"

Clifford says with a cheer.

And into the sunset,

The three disappear.

BOOKS IN THIS SERIES:

Welcome to Birdwell Island: Everyone on Birdwell Island thinks that Clifford is just too big! But when there's an emergency, Clifford The Big Red Dog teaches everyone to have respect—even for those who are different.

A Puppy to Love: Emily Elizabeth's birthday wish comes true: She gets a puppy to love! And with her love and kindness, Clifford The Small Red Puppy becomes Clifford The Big Red Dog!

The Big Sleep Over: Clifford has to spend his first night without Emily Elizabeth. When he has trouble falling asleep, his Birdwell Island friends work together to make sure that he—and everyone else—gets a good night's sleep.

No Dogs Allowed: No dogs in Birdwell Island Park? That's what Mr. Bleakman says—before he realizes that sharing the park with dogs is much more fun.

An Itchy Day: Clifford has an itchy patch! He's afraid to go to the vet, so he tries to hide his scratching from Emily Elizabeth. But Clifford soon realizes that it's better to be truthful and trust the person he loves most— Emily Elizabeth.

The Doggy Detectives: Oh, no! Emily Elizabeth is accused of stealing Jetta's gold medal—and then her shiny mirror! But her dear Clifford never doubts her innocence and, with his fellow doggy detectives, finds the real thief.

Follow the Leader: While playing follow-the-leader with Clifford and T-Bone, Cleo learns that playing fair is the best way to play!

The Big Red Mess: Clifford tries to stay clean for the Dog of the Year contest, but he ends up becoming a big red mess! However, when Clifford helps the judge reach the shore safely, he finds that he doesn't need to stay clean to be the Dog of the Year.

The Big Surprise: Poor Clifford. It's his birthday, but none of his friends will play with him. Maybe it's because they're all busy. . . planning his surprise party!

The Wild Ice Cream Machine: Charley and Emily Elizabeth decide to work the ice cream machine themselves. Things go smoothly. . . until the lever gets stuck and they find themselves knee-deep in ice cream!

Dogs and Cats: Can dogs and cats be friends? Clifford, T-Bone, and Cleo don't think so. But they have a change of heart after they help two lost kittens find their mother.

The Magic Ball: Emily Elizabeth trusts Clifford to deliver a package to the post office, but he opens it and breaks the gift inside. Clifford tries to hide his blunder, but Emily Elizabeth appreciates honesty and understands that accidents happen.